ATLANTIS SQUAREPANTIS

adapted by Erica Pass
based on the teleplay by Dani Michaeli and Steven Banks
illustrated by The Artifact Group

ADVANCE PUBLISHERS

Stephen Hillenburg

Based on the TV series *SpongeBob SquarePants*® created by Stephen Hillenburg as seen on Nickelodeon®

Advance Publishers, L.C.
1060 Maitland Center Commons, Suite 365
Maitland, FL 32751 USA

©2009 Viacom International Inc. All Rights Reserved. Nickelodeon, SpongeBob SquarePants
and all related titles, logos and characters are trademarks of Viacom International Inc.
All rights reserved, including the right of reproduction in whole or in part in any form.
Manufactured in China
10 9 8 7 6 5 4 3 2 1
ISBN-10: 1-57973-376-X

It was a perfect day for blowing bubbles. SpongeBob blew a bubble large
and floaty enough to carry him and Patrick high above Bikini Bottom.

"This bubble will break all records," said SpongeBob. But he didn't realize how
far they had gone until much later.

The two began to pound on the bubble. "We're never going to get out of
here!" they cried.

The bubble finally coasted down and into a cave, coming to rest against something sharp. It burst, and Patrick and SpongeBob fell to the ground.

"What happened?" asked Patrick.

"*That's* what happened!" said SpongeBob, pointing at a jagged piece of metal. He got closer and saw that it said "Antis."

"What do you think that means, Pat?"

"Hmm," said Patrick. "Antis . . . antis . . . SquarePantis! It probably belonged to your ancestors! You must wear the ancient crest of your ancestors, for it is your birthright!"

And Patrick stuck the amulet in SpongeBob's head!

SpongeBob and Patrick decided to take it to the Bikini Bottom Museum, where they bumped into Squidward.

"Would you two watch where you're—," Squidward started to yell. Then he saw what SpongeBob had in his hand. "What are you doing with the amulet of Atlantis?" he asked. He thought they were trying to steal it from the museum!

But then Squidward realized that SpongeBob and Patrick had in fact found the missing half of the Atlantian amulet!

"What's an Atlantian omelet?" asked SpongeBob.

"Amulet!" yelled Squidward. "Not omelet! It's the key to untold riches!"

At that moment Mr. Krabs showed up. "Did someone say 'untold riches'?"

Squidward told them about the lost city of Atlantis. "For reasons unknown, the great city disappeared one day, and no ruins were ever found. All the inventions you take for granted were given to us by the Atlantians."

As Squidward spoke, SpongeBob found himself staring at a bubble shown on a mural. He pointed it out to Patrick.

"That's the oldest living bubble," said Squidward. "It lives in Atlantis."

"It's the most beautiful bubble I've ever seen," said Patrick.

Just then Sandy showed up. "What's all the hubbub, boys?" she asked.

"These two chowderbrains found the missing half of the amulet of Atlantis," said Squidward.

"Well, let's hitch them two doggies up!" said Sandy.

The group watched as Squidward carefully placed the two pieces together— and they glowed!

Suddenly there was a bright beam of light and lots of rumbling—and a huge van appeared, crashing through the ceiling of the museum! The amulet began to spin. It rose up and landed in a slot on the front of the van. The doors opened up.

"Welcome aboard the sea ship *Atlantis*," a computerized voice said. "This is a nonstop trip, so please take a seat, relax, and we'll be on our way."

RING FOR THE KING

The gang coasted deep through the water until finally they could see Atlantis below. Then they hurtled toward the city and hit the ground, skidding to a stop. They emerged from the van and approached a long staircase. At the bottom was a bell.

"Go on, SpongeBob," said Mr. Krabs. "Ring the bell."

RING
FOR
THE
KING

SpongeBob rang the bell and everyone waited nervously as a red carpet
rolled down the stairs.

"Welcome to Atlantis," a voice announced. "I've been expecting you."

With that, someone tumbled down the stairs, arriving at SpongeBob's feet.
"Allow me to introduce myself," he said. "I am the Lord Royal Highness. But my
friends call me LRH."

"My friends call me SpongeBob," said SpongeBob. "I'm here to see the oldest
bubble."

Meanwhile Plankton had snuck aboard the bus after he overheard the group talking about the collection of weapons in Atlantis.

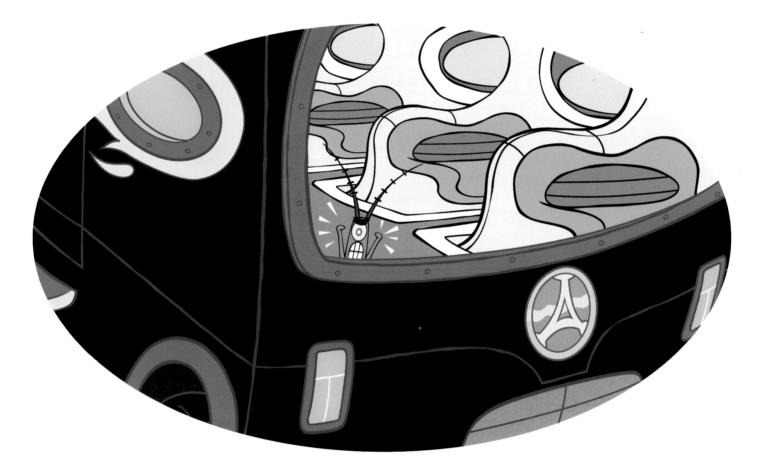

LRH happily showed SpongeBob and his friends around the city. "For centuries, we Atlantians spent our talents and energy building weapons to defend ourselves," he said. "But we gave up the idea of warfare long ago, and now these weapons gather dust behind these locked doors–to show what must be done if one wishes to live in harmony with all creatures of this or any world."

Next they came upon a room filled with treasure.
"Long ago we decided to focus on gathering knowledge instead of wealth,"
said LRH. The group followed him away from the riches, except for Mr. Krabs.

Sandy was looking forward to seeing some Atlantian inventions.
"Of course," LRH said. "I give you the Atlantian Hall of Science!"
"Hoppin' acorns!" said Sandy when she saw the room filled with machines.
One machine even took objects and turned them into ice cream!
Sandy decided to stay behind in the Hall of Science.

At the Hall of Arts, Squidward couldn't believe his eyes. "The creativity! The artistry!" he cried out. "Looks like I'll be here inspiring these Atlantian art makers with my beauty. You guys go on ahead!"

"Excuse me, sir," SpongeBob said to LRH. "Can we see the bubble now?"

"Of course you can!" said LRH. "But first, please remember the bubble is more than one million years old."

SpongeBob and Patrick ran toward the bubble, which was held within a large glass ball.

"So ancient, so floaty," said SpongeBob admiringly. "It's the most beautiful, wrinkled-up, dusty old bubble I've ever seen."

"Like a delicate air raisin!" said Patrick.

LRH had to get ready for dinner. "I'm going to leave you two friendly strangers alone with our most beloved, ancient, and fragile Atlantian relic," he said as he walked away.

In their excitement, SpongeBob and Patrick pushed against the glass ball and set it loose. They struggled under its weight, finally setting it straight. And the bubble had not burst!

"That was a close one, buddy," said SpongeBob. "We should go before something else happens."

"Let's get a picture for our scrapbooks before we leave," said Patrick.
"Great idea, Pat!" SpongeBob agreed.
But it turned out to be anything *but* a great idea when the flash from the camera made the bubble burst!

SpongeBob and Patrick were panicking when they arrived for dinner. "We have to go back to Bikini Bottom now," they said.

"Why would you want to leave a paradise like this?" Squidward asked.

"Because," said SpongeBob, stalling, "I miss Gary . . . and–"

"We destroyed your most prized possession!" Patrick blurted out.

SpongeBob and Patrick were ready for LRH to start yelling at them.

But instead, LRH simply admitted, "That's not the real bubble. It's just a prop for the tourists!"

He took out a small jar with a wrinkled bubble floating inside. "This is the real deal," he said proudly.

"Ooohh," said SpongeBob and Patrick, relieved and thrilled at the same time. Then Patrick took another picture—and the bubble burst!

This time LRH was furious. "Summon the royal guard!" he roared. "Seize the hostile bubble poppers!"

"Let's hightail it out of here!" called Sandy.

With the guards chasing them, the Bikini Bottom gang ran—until they crashed into a large tank.

Suddenly a voice from inside the machine announced, "1 am in control of the most powerful weapon in Atlantis! Now bow before the new king of Atlantis, and prepare to taste my wrath!"

It was Plankton! He hopped on a button and . . . SPLURT! Ice cream oozed onto everyone below.

"Mmm . . . thanks, Plankton!" Patrick said between mouthfuls of ice cream. Plankton jumped out of the machine and kicked it, muttering to himself.

LRH was delighted. "Look, a talking speck!" he said. "It will make a fantastic replacement for our recently deflated national treasure."

As Plankton ranted and raved in a jar, LRH said good-bye to the visitors from Bikini Bottom. He seemed very eager to see them leave.

"So nice to meet you all," said LRH. "I hope you have a safe journey home. Do come back anytime."